You Choose Stories: Wonder Woman
is published by Stone Arch Books,
A Capstone Imprint
1710 Roe Crest Drive
North Mankato, Minnesota 56003
www.capstonepub.com

STAR41681

Library of Congress Cataloging-in-Publication Data is
available on the Library of Congress website.
ISBN: 978-1-4965-8350-5 (library binding)
ISBN: 978-1-4965-8440-3 (paperback)
ISBN: 978-1-4965-8355-0 (eBook PDF)

Summary: Circe vows revenge when she is offended by
her character being cut from a remake of *The Odyssey*. When
Wonder Woman tries to stop her, the sorceress creates portals
that take the hero into magical movie worlds. Now it's up
to you to help her defeat Circe's *Movie Magic Madness*!

Editor: Christopher Harbo

Designer: Hilary Wacholz

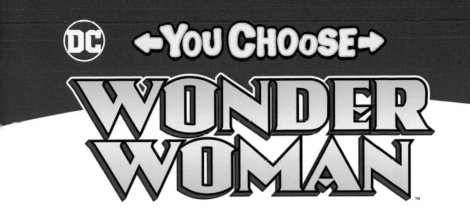

MOVIE MAGIC MADNESS

written by
Michael Anthony Steele

illustrated by
Omar Lozano

Wonder Woman created by
William Moulton Marston

STONE ARCH BOOKS
a capstone imprint

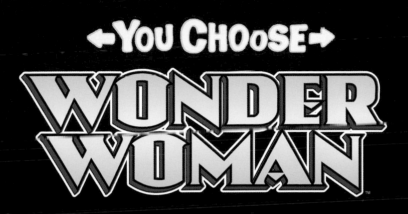

Circe vows revenge when she is offended
by her character being cut from a remake of
The Odyssey. When Wonder Woman tries to
stop her, the sorceress creates portals that
take the hero into magical movie worlds. Now
it's up to you to help her defeat Circe's *Movie
Magic Madness!*

Follow the directions at the bottom of
each page. The choices YOU make will change
the outcome of the story. After you finish one
path, go back and read the others for more
Wonder Woman adventures!

Wonder Woman floats high above the clouds. She scans the horizon but sees no one else around. She seems to be alone, but she knows that she's not.

"I do not wish to fight you!" Wonder Woman shouts. She crosses her arms and sighs. "I only want you to return to your home."

WHOOOOOOSH!

An enormous red bird bursts from the clouds below. The giant creature slams into the Amazon warrior, sending her tumbling through the sky. Wonder Woman quickly recovers and clenches her fists. She readies for battle as the bird circles around for another attack.

SKREEE! The phoenix screeches and closes in.

Wonder Woman often finds herself fighting mythical beasts. Some are released by villains for evil plots. Others simply wander into the world of man by themselves. This magical phoenix is one of those wanderers.

Turn the page.

SKREEE!

The phoenix swoops in and slashes at Wonder Woman with its sharp talons. The hero crosses her arms, and sparks fly as claws strike the Amazon's silver bracelets.

"Don't say I didn't warn you," Wonder Woman says. Then she swoops behind the beast, grabs its flapping wings, and plants her feet on the bird's back. Unable to fly, the phoenix and Wonder Woman plummet toward the ocean below.

As the water beneath them draws closer and closer, the bird's wings suddenly grow warm in her hands.

"Fires of Hades," Wonder Woman says, holding the now red-hot bird. "You don't have to do this."

SKREEE! The creature cries out once more before erupting into flames. The magical blaze swallows both the bird and the hero. The fireball flares like a second sun. When the flames finally fade, only Wonder Woman remains.

The hero shakes her head and glances at the thin trail of ash dancing on the wind.

"I don't know if you can hear me," Wonder Woman tells the ashes. "But when you rise again, remain in your own lands and we'll have no quarrel."

Wonder Woman knows the phoenix will rise again from its ashes. She just hopes that it will listen to her advice when it does.

Wonder Woman turns to head toward shore, and then she spots trouble on the beach below.

"Mighty Odysseus," she says. "Now what?"

Wonder Woman can't believe her eyes. Yet another mythical creature is loose in the world. A giant Cyclops looms over a group of people. The one-eyed creature raises an enormous club, ready to strike.

"Hermes give me speed," Wonder Woman says as she races toward the beach.

Turn the page.

The Amazon arrives just in time. She swoops in and catches the giant club just before it strikes the people on the beach.

"Cut!" shouts a loud voice. Wonder Woman looks down to see a man with a bullhorn running across the sand. "What's going on here?!"

"Take cover," orders Wonder Woman, raising a fist to strike. "I'll handle this beast."

"Don't you dare," says the man. "Do you know how much that thing costs?"

Wonder Woman holds her attack. She glances up and sees two large cranes hovering over the creature. Thick cables running down from the cranes are attached to the Cyclops's shoulders. They control the creature like a huge puppet.

The Amazon warrior releases the club and drifts down the beach. Along the way, she spots a group of men and women around a movie camera. Nearby, a man holds a microphone at the end of a long pole.

Wonder Woman realizes her mistake.

"Ah, I see now," she says. "You're making a movie here, aren't you?"

"You guessed it," replies the man with the bullhorn. "I'm directing a remake of the Greek epic, *The Odyssey*."

"Of course," says Wonder Woman. She smiles and points up to the robotic giant. "And that must be Polyphemus, the Cyclops from the story."

"You sure know your Greek mythology," says the director.

"I know some," she says with a sly smile. If only the director knew that Wonder Woman has actually met, helped, or fought most of the creatures of myth.

"Well, you're welcome to stay and **SNORT** if you want," the director says.

The Amazon raises an eyebrow. "Excuse me?"

The director's eyes widen as he covers his face. "I . . . I don't know why I just did that."

"That's quite all right," Wonder Woman replies. "Everyone makes mistakes . . ."

Turn the page.

The director interrupts her with a loud **SQUEAL!** He lowers his hands and his nose is now flat and round. It looks just like a pig's nose.

"What's—**SQUEAL!**—happening—**SNORT?!**" The director transforms into a pig right before Wonder Woman's eyes.

"Great Hera," Wonder Woman says as she scans the crowd. The whole movie crew is transforming too. When the changes are complete, snorting, squealing pigs run wild on the beach.

The crazy scene reminds Wonder Woman of another character from *The Odyssey*. In the book, a powerful sorceress also turned the heroes into pigs—and Wonder Woman has battled her many times.

Wonder Woman scans the area. "You can come out now, Circe," she says. "This looks like your handiwork."

"Ha-ha-ha-ha-ha-ha!" Laughter fills the air. "Princess Diana of Themyscira. Wonder Woman. I'm flattered you remember me."

Circe appears in a flash of purple light. The sorceress hovers above Wonder Woman, peering down at her with icy blue eyes.

"Restore these people at once," Diana orders.

"Let me think—no!" Circe grins, her purple hair swirling around her head. "Did you know they cut my character out of their little movie?"

"That's no reason to turn them into pigs," Wonder Woman says. She rises off the beach, up toward the floating sorceress.

"I think it is," Circe says as she points to the giant Cyclops.

The robotic Cyclops begins to glow. Suddenly it comes to life and breaks free from its cables. The ground shakes as it runs toward Wonder Woman.

"It's going to take more than a movie magic monster to defeat me," the Amazon warrior says.

As the robot swings its club, Diana leaps into the air and delivers a mighty kick.

WHACK!

Turn the page.

The Cyclops flies backward as it shatters into a million metal pieces.

"*Movie* magic?" asks the sorceress with an evil grin. "What a delicious idea!" Circe disappears in a flash of light.

"Get back here, Circe!" Diana shouts. "You can't leave these people like this."

Just then, a magical portal appears. It floats a few inches above the ground.

"Come and find me, Princess," says Circe's voice. "Let's play."

"I hate going blind into one of Circe's traps," Wonder Woman says to herself. "But if I'm going to save the movie crew, I don't have a choice."

"You want a choice?" Circe asks. "Why didn't you say so?"

In a flash of light, the magical portal divides into three. Now a red, a blue, and a yellow portal each float above the sand.

If Wonder Woman enters the red portal, turn to page 16.
If Wonder Woman enters the blue portal, turn to page 44.
If Wonder Woman enters the yellow portal, turn to page 73.

Wonder Woman enters the red portal and suddenly finds herself in the middle of a medieval village under attack. Villagers run screaming while burning huts light up the night.

"Merciful Minerva," Diana says. "Where have you taken me, Circe?"

Wonder Woman is about to spring into action when she notices her change of clothing. She now wears her battle armor, complete with sword and shield.

A young man runs up to her. "Thank heavens you're here, brave knight," he says. "For we would have fallen if not for your arrival."

"I'm sorry," says Wonder Woman. "What's—"

ROOOOOOOOOARRRRRR!!!

The hero looks up and sees a giant dragon flying across the sky. It flaps its wings and seems to smile down on the destruction below.

The beast takes a deep breath and blasts a column of fire toward the village. More huts erupt in flames as the villagers run for their lives.

"Looks like Circe placed me in the middle of a fantasy movie," says Wonder Woman. "She wasn't kidding about movie magic."

A young girl screams as the wall of a burning building tips toward her. Wonder Woman becomes a blur as she runs toward the girl and scoops her up. She carries her to safety as the burning wall smashes to the ground.

"Fantasy or not, these people should not be terrorized," Wonder Woman says as she grips her sword tightly.

The hero is about to fly up and attack the dragon when the girl takes her arm. "Only the wizard can defeat the dragon," the girl says.

"Wizard?" asks Diana. "What wizard?"

The girl points over Wonder Woman's left shoulder. The hero turns to see a giant black castle looming over the village.

"He lives in the castle," the girl explains.

If Wonder Woman attacks the dragon, turn to page 18.
If Wonder Woman asks the wizard for help, turn to page 29.

ROOOOOOOOARRRRR!!!

The dragon swoops in for another attack. It blasts the village with another stream of fire.

"I don't know what game Circe is playing," Wonder Woman says. "But now is not the time to seek out wizards."

Diana launches into the air, flying toward the flames. She positions herself between the dragon and the village. She raises her shield, blocking the stream of fire. The shield grows red-hot.

"How do you like this kind of movie magic?" Circe's voice asks.

Wonder Woman glances around, but she doesn't spot the sorceress. Then she notices the dragon hovering above her. A wide grin stretches across its face. "Realistic special effects, huh?" asks the dragon, but in Circe's voice.

The Amazon flies up to join the dragon. "This isn't fun, Circe."

"Are you sure?" The Circe dragon chuckles. "I'm having fun."

The dragon blasts Wonder Woman with another stream of deadly fire. As before, Diana blocks the attack with her shield.

"Let's see how you like this then," Wonder Woman says. She raises her sword and charges the winged beast. She strikes the dragon's shoulder, but her blade bounces off the creature's hard scales.

"Sorry. Not good enough," says Circe.

The Circe dragon whips its tail around and slams it into the Amazon. **BAM!** Wonder Woman tumbles down into the forest beyond the village. Her body smashes through large trees and comes to a stop against a huge boulder.

Wonder Woman gets to her feet and sneers at the circling dragon. "This ends now, evil sorceress."

Suddenly, the ground trembles beneath Wonder Woman's feet. She turns and spots a cloud of dust in the west. Something big is moving toward the village.

If Wonder Woman investigates the dust cloud, turn to page 20.
If Wonder Woman continues to fight the dragon, turn to page 26.

"What has that sorceress planned for me now?" Wonder Woman asks as the rumbling grows louder.

Suddenly, huge trees crumple over and a cloud of debris fills the air. The dust settles to reveal a huge orc army. Hundreds of the vicious creatures carry swords, shields, clubs, and spears. Others haul large war machines like catapults and giant crossbows. A big and particularly mean looking orc leads the way. He wears a horned helmet and carries a battle-ax.

"What is this?" The orc snarls. "Village send just one little human to fight?" He laughs and points to Wonder Woman. "One against . . . ," he begins to count his companions. "One, two, three, four, five, six . . . well . . . a lot more!"

"I do not wish to fight any of you," the hero says. "But I can't let you attack that village."

The orc leader scratches his head and shrugs. "Me don't understand. Dragon says to attack the village. So we have to fight." He raises a finger. "I know! Just me will fight you!"

The orc hoists his battle-ax over his head and attacks. Wonder Woman raises her sword and blocks the blow.

KLANG!

The orc leader growls as he raises his ax for another chop. When his weapon is high, Diana slams her shield against the orc's chest.

POW!

The orc leader flies back and tumbles across the ground. The other orcs grumble in frustration, but they don't jump into the battle.

"I thought orcs were smart," Wonder Woman says with grin.

"Orcs *very* smart," the orc leader says as he gets to his feet. "Don't me sound smart? Me speak very goodly." He swings his ax at Wonder Woman. She easily ducks out of the way.

The orc growls and swings again.

"I don't know," says Wonder Woman. She easily blocks the blow with her shield. "It's not very smart to take orders from a dragon."

Turn to page 23.

The orc leader freezes in mid strike. He tilts his head to one side. "It's not?" he asks.

Diana shakes her head. "No, it's not. Everyone knows that."

The huge orc lowers his ax. "If everyone knows it, then orcs know it. Orcs are very smart."

Wonder Woman smiles. "Yes, you did just say that."

The orc leader turns to his army. "Orcs have new plan. Attack the dragon!"

The Circe dragon had circled lower to watch the fight. Now she is in easy range of all the orc weapons. The giant crossbows shoot huge arrows, while the catapults launch balls of fire.

"What are you doing?" Circe asks. "What's going on down there?"

The Circe dragon dodges the arrows but is pelted with flaming boulders. The dragon inhales, about to blast the orcs with fire. Luckily, one of the huge rocks slams into her head.

BAM!

Turn the page.

The dragon cries out and then tumbles toward the ground. It lands in a heap on the forest floor.

FWOOM!

Wonder Woman flies over to the downed dragon. The beast tries to stand but is too weak and dizzy. The orcs are not far behind. They scream battle cries as they charge toward the injured beast.

"They'll be here soon," Wonder Woman says. "Don't you think you've had enough of this movie magic?"

The Circe dragon rolls its eyes and lets out a sigh. "Fine."

The beast raises a huge paw and snaps its bony fingers. In a flash of light, Wonder Woman stands on the beach again. Circe stands next to her.

Wonder Woman crosses her arms and raises an eyebrow. "Aren't you forgetting something, Circe?"

The sorceress sighs and rolls her eyes.

"Fine," Circe says again. She snaps her fingers and there's a flash of purple light, and then everyone is back to normal. The sorceress restores the entire movie crew.

Diana nods approvingly. "You did the right thing, Circe."

The villain rolls her eyes and waves her away. "Yeah, whatevs."

The director staggers up to Wonder Woman and Circe. "That was weird," he says, shaking his head. "I don't know what happened there."

"I'll tell you what happened," the hero says as she places a hand on Circe's shoulder. "That was my friend here trying out for the part of Circe." Diana smiles at the sorceress. "I think you'll find she can help with your special effects too."

Circe's eyes light up with excitement.

THE END

To follow another path, turn to page 15.

"I don't know what Circe has planned for me next," Wonder Woman says. "But there's only one way to stop it."

Diana takes to the air again. Her sword and shield at the ready, she attacks the dragon once more.

CLINK! CLANK! CLINK!

Unfortunately, no matter where she strikes, her sword bounces off the dragon's hard scales.

Wonder Woman raises her shield just in time as the Circe dragon fights back with another fireball.

WHOOOOSH! The shield gets red-hot under the blaze.

Once the flames are spent, Diana shakes her head. "My sword is of no use," she says as she sheathes her weapon. "I'll have to think of something else."

Wonder Woman pulls the golden lasso from her hip. As she uncoils the rope, the dragon lunges for her.

When the dragon snaps its mouth at Wonder Woman, the hero sends a loop over the creature's snout. Diana pulls the lasso tight, keeping the dragon's jaws shut.

The Circe dragon's eyes widen with panic. It begins to claw at the magical rope, but Wonder Woman is too fast. She flies around the dragon, tying its front claws up against its long neck. The beast wriggles, trying to break free, but the rope is too strong.

Wonder Woman's magic lasso, the Lasso of Truth, makes anyone it binds tell the truth. Diana looks into the dragon's eyes and focuses the lasso's power.

"Are you truly a dragon?" the hero asks.

The dragon sighs. "No," it replies through clenched teeth.

FLASH! In a burst of light the dragon transforms back into Circe. Still wrapped in the golden lasso, the sorceress floats in the air next to Wonder Woman.

Turn the page.

"Are we truly in a fantasy movie?" asks Diana.

Circe glares at the Amazon. "No," she replies.

FLASH! Wonder Woman and Circe no longer hover in the night sky. The sky is blue and seagulls soar through the air. They're back at the beach.

Wonder Woman and Circe float down to the shore below. Once on the ground, Diana points to the pigs running through the sand. "Are these animals truly pigs?"

Circe sighs. "No."

FLASH! All of the scampering pigs return to their human forms.

The director stumbles up toward Wonder Woman. "What's going on?" he asks her.

"Just some dark magic," Diana replies. She turns to Circe. "And a trip to Themyscira for some Amazonian justice."

THE END

To follow another path, turn to page 15.

Wonder Woman flies toward the nearby castle. "If it helps restore the movie crew to their human forms, I'll play Circe's game for now," she says.

The hero lands in front of the main entrance. The castle is sealed by two thick wooden doors. Diana summons all of her strength and shoves against them.

CREEEK-CRACK! The doors crack and splinter as they finally give way. Once the shattered doors are pushed aside, she strolls inside.

As soon as she's inside the castle courtyard, the ground rumbles beneath her feet. Then plumes of dirt erupt around her. Bony hands reach through the earth. They pull at the ground, hauling up skeleton warriors behind them. Soon, eight bony soldiers surround Wonder Woman. They hold rusty swords and shields, and they glare at her through empty eye sockets.

"Of course." Diana rolls her eyes. "What fantasy movie isn't complete without skeleton warriors?"

Turn the page.

The skeleton soldiers hiss as they move in for the attack. Wonder Woman deflects their blows with her shield and swipes at them with her own blade. **KLINK-KLINK! KLANK!** They block her blows and drive her back toward the base of a tall tower.

Wonder Woman strikes one of the skeletons with her blade. When she does, the bones fall apart and clatter to the ground. She quickly takes out three more skeletons the same way. Then the rest drive her through an opening in the tower.

Diana runs up a spiral staircase to gain the higher ground. After a few steps, she turns and faces the pursuing skeletons. They clash swords some more until she gets in another successful blow. Bones bounce and rattle down the stone stairs after she defeats another. Now only three bony warriors drive her onward and upward.

By the time Wonder Woman reaches the top of the tower, only two skeletons remain. Although still outnumbered, Diana is confident she can defeat the last two bony soldiers.

Turn to page 32.

"Oh, dear," says a voice behind her.

Diana glances back to see an old man with a long gray beard. He wears dark robes and holds a carved wooden staff.

"You must be the wizard," Diana says. She turns back just in time to block a blow from one of the skeletons.

"Yes," replies the man. "And those guards weren't for you, I'm afraid."

The wizard taps his staff on the ground. **TZZZAP!** Electricity sparks from the top of the wood, and the skeletons crumple to the ground.

Diana finds herself standing over a heap of old bones and rusty weapons. She nudges one of the empty helmets with her boot. "Who were they for?" she asks.

The wizard points out the window toward the dragon circling in the distance. "Why, they were for the sorceress, of course," he says. "The wielder of dark magic who created this world. The one who now pretends to be a dragon."

Diana raises an eyebrow. "You know about Circe?" she asks.

The man shrugs. "If she creates a fantastical world with fellow magic-users, then a wizard such as myself would surely know this."

"But why would she . . . ," Diana begins.

"Create someone who could defeat her?" the wizard finishes. He holds up a finger and grins.

"Circe has to follow the rules of the worlds she creates," the wizard explains. He smiles and nods slowly. "You would be wise to remember that fact."

"Thank you for the advice," Wonder Woman says. "But do you happen know how I can beat her right now?"

"Of course," says the wizard. "Some say you must fight fire with fire." The top of his staff begins to glow. "But I say you should fight fire with ice!"

TZZZAP!

Turn the page.

More electric sparks erupt from the top of his staff, and a large ice dragon appears just outside the tower window. It slowly flaps its wings as it hovers in midair.

"Your mighty steed awaits, brave knight," the wizard says with a bow.

"Thank you," says Wonder Woman. She's about to exit the window when she spots a nearby door. Purple light glows around it. "What's in there?" she asks.

"Nothing of value in this world," the man replies with a sigh. "Another one of the sorceress's traps I'm afraid."

If Wonder Woman climbs onto the dragon, turn to page 35.
If Wonder Woman investigates the door, turn to page 38.

Wonder Woman steps out of the window and climbs onto the dragon's back. The beast is cold, and its wings make clinking sounds as they flap. The magical creature really is made of ice. As soon as Diana grips its neck, the beast takes off. It soars toward the Circe dragon.

Diana strokes the creature's shoulder. "May the fates be with us, my friend."

As they close in on the Circe dragon, Diana notices a dust cloud on the ground. She leans over and spots an orc army advancing toward the village.

"Care to warm up on some orcs?" she asks the dragon.

The ice dragon snorts as it dives toward the forest. As it nears the mass of monsters, it opens its mouth wide. A column of ice pours from the dragon's jaws. The frigid stream blasts the orcs as they fly over. The advancing army's feet are frozen in place.

"Now, it's Circe's turn," says Diana.

Turn the page.

"I don't think so, Princess," booms Circe's voice from above.

Wonder Woman barely has time to turn her dragon as the Circe dragon moves in. A stream of flames erupts from its mouth. The ice dragon isn't lucky enough to dodge the attack completely. The fire washes over the dragon's tail, melting it completely.

"I wonder if that wizard had the right idea using an ice dragon to fight fire," Diana says.

She turns her dragon to fly at Circe head-on. As the two dragons near each other, both open their mouths. Circe shoots out a column of flames while Wonder Woman's dragon blasts ice.

As soon as the two streams meet, the column of ice puts out the fire. The stream of ice pushes all the way through the flames and into the Circe dragon's mouth. She coughs and gags, unable to speak.

"It's about time you had nothing to say," says Wonder Woman.

Her dragon blasts the Circe dragon again. This time the ice washes over every inch of the beast. Now frozen in a block of ice, the Circe dragon tumbles toward the ground.

Wonder Woman readies her lasso as her dragon follows. But her dragon isn't fast enough. The frozen block holding the Circe dragon hits the ground and shatters into a million pieces.

WHOOSH!

After a flash of light, Wonder Woman finds herself standing on the beach again. Circe sits on the sand in front of her, and the members of the movie crew are no longer pigs.

Circe looks up and snarls at the Amazon. She tries to speak but nothing comes out.

"Don't worry, Circe," Wonder Woman says with a grin. "I'm sure your voice will return in time for your trial."

THE END

To follow another path, turn to page 15.

Wonder Woman's curiosity gets the best of her. "What is that wizard hiding?" she asks as she walks toward the mysterious door.

"Don't say I didn't warn you," the wizard says.

Diana opens the door to see blinding light beyond. She can't make out any details, but she steps through anyway.

"Captain on the bridge," says a man's voice.

Wonder Woman blinks and finds herself on the bridge of a starship while several crew members stand at attention. Diana looks down to see she now wears a sleek uniform. Her sword and shield are gone.

"What's going on?" she asks.

"The leader of the Hartunians is demanding to speak with you," says a man with blue skin. He points to a large view screen showing an alien ship floating in space.

"Hartunians?" Wonder Woman asks.

Suddenly the screen is filled with a close-up of Circe's face. "Hello, Captain," she says.

Turn to page 40.

Diana steps closer to the view screen. "What is this?" she asks. "A science fiction movie?"

"Surrender now, Diana," Circe continues. "Or be blown to bits!"

Suddenly, everyone sways to the left as the ship rocks under their feet. "The Hartunian ship fired on us," reports the blue man. "But the shields are holding."

"Don't worry, I can easily destroy your ship," Circe says. "Or you can save your crew and accept the Hartunian trial by combat."

"I'm surprised you would challenge me to combat," Wonder Woman says. "You must have some trickery in mind."

"Not at all," Circe says. "It's simple. Someone from my ship versus someone from your ship."

Wonder Woman looks past Circe. The crew members on her ship are small, green-skinned aliens. They would be easy to best in battle. But still . . .

If Wonder Woman takes her chances with her ship, turn to page 41.

If Wonder Woman chooses trial by combat, turn to page 95.

Diana shakes her head. "I don't trust you, Circe." She looks at the blue-skinned man and points to the view screen. "Can you turn that screen off?"

"End transmission," the man says, pressing a button. Circe disappears from the screen

"Look, Captain!" One of the crew members points to the main screen. Several spindly-legged robots stream out of the enemy ship. "Hartunian spider-bots," he says. "They'll get under our shields and rip our ship to shreds."

"Captain!" The blue man stands at attention. "Permission to lead a team to fight off those spider-bots?"

Diana knows when to play along. "Permission granted," she replies. "But I'm going with you."

Wonder Woman follows the crew members to the access hatch. Even though she doesn't need one, she pulls on a spacesuit like the others. She attaches her magic golden lasso to the outside of her suit.

Turn the page.

Once everyone is ready, the blue man opens the hatch. Diana leads the way out of the ship.

Outside, the crew members use laser pistols to blast away at the spider-bots. Wonder Woman doesn't bother with that. Instead, she remembers what the wizard told her. Circe has to play by the rules of the world she created.

"I wonder if *I* have to play by the same rules," she says to herself.

Wonder Woman flies past her crew members and grabs a spider-bot in each hand.

POW! The robots explode when she smashes them together. Diana smiles. She can still fly, and she still has superhuman strength.

"I think I found my secret weapon," she says.

With the speed of Hermes, Wonder Woman zips around the outside of the ship. She scoops up each of the spider-bots and crumples them into a ball. Then she hurls the ball at Circe's starship. The ball of bots smashes through one of the ship's engines.

KA-BOOM!

The engine explodes, and the enemy ship drifts out of control.

Wonder Woman flies closer as escape pods shoot out from the dying ship. The Amazon spots one pod in particular and readies her magic lasso. She loops the pod before it disappears into space. Diana hauls the pod closer to see an angry Circe glaring at her through the window.

Diana wraps her lasso around the escape pod. "I know you can't come out unless you take us back to our world," Diana explains. "And when you do, I'll have you trapped."

Circe snarls. "I can wait!"

Diana smiles and crosses her arms. She knows Circe isn't a very patient person.

THE END

To follow another path, turn to page 15.

FLASH!

After a burst of light, Wonder Woman finds herself standing in a small rustic town. She moves forward and hears **CLINK, CLINK, CLINK** with each step.

Diana looks down to see that she now wears spurs on the back of tall cowboy boots. Her golden lasso still hangs from one hip, but she now wears jeans and a leather jacket. A large black cowboy hat shades her eyes from the sun.

"Circe really meant what she said about movie magic," Diana says to herself. "She put me in the middle of an old western."

As Wonder Woman walks down the dusty street, men on horseback sneer at her as they ride by. People on the sidewalk point at her and whisper. Others run inside buildings and slam shut doors and windows. It seems as if the entire town is wary of her.

Diana spots a piece of paper flapping on a signpost. She marches over for a closer look. It's a wanted poster with her photo on it.

"Dangerous Diana," Wonder Woman reads. "Wanted dead or alive. Five hundred dollar reward." The hero glances around and spots more wanted posters flapping on posts all over town.

"No wonder everyone is looking at me so strangely. Circe set me up as the bad guy in this movie," Wonder Woman says. She leaves the poster and continues down the street. "Maybe I should talk to the town sheriff about that."

Wonder Woman heads to the sidewalk. "Excuse me," she asks a woman carrying a parcel. "Where is the sheriff's office?"

The woman looks down, turns away, and disappears into a nearby shop. Diana turns to another group of people, but they scatter before she can get a word out.

"Circe has them terrified of me," Wonder Woman says.

Suddenly, a rope wraps around the hero's waist. **YANK!** A sharp tug jerks her off the sidewalk and into the middle of the street.

Turn the page.

Wonder Woman looks up. A man on a horse has the other end of the rope. He backs his horse up, pulling the rope tighter.

"You do not want to do this, friend," Wonder Woman tells him.

The man doesn't reply. Instead, he waves over two other cowboys. "Come on, boys!" he shouts. "Let's get us that reward!"

The others ride up and lasso Wonder Woman with their own ropes. They ride in a circle around the hero, the ropes tightening as they go.

"I tried to warn you," Wonder Woman says. She flies into the air, pulling the cowboys from their horses. Then she spins in midair, twirling the cowboys around like a merry-go-round.

"Whoa!" they shout as they let go of the ropes. Each cowboy flies off in a different direction.

KRASH! KRASH! Two cowboys crash through shop windows.

SPLOOSH! One lands in a nearby watering trough.

Wonder Woman shrugs off the ropes and floats down to the soaked cowboy. She unhooks her own lasso and loops it around the man.

"Where is the sheriff's office?" she asks. The cowboy is terrified, but the magic lasso makes him tell the truth.

"Over there!" the cowboy says. He points to a building at the end of the street.

Wonder Woman releases the cowboy. She coils her lasso as she marches down the street toward the sheriff's office.

"I don't know what kind of story Circe has in mind," she says. "But I have no wish to be labeled a criminal."

Diana enters the sheriff's office to see a figure sitting at a desk. A shiny star is pinned to the sheriff's shirt. A large white hat hides the sheriff's face.

"Excuse me, Sheriff," says Diana. "I'd like to talk to you about the wanted posters you have all over town."

Turn the page.

"Happy to help in any way I can, ma'am," says a familiar voice. The sheriff pushes back her white hat to reveal—

"Circe!" Wonder Woman says. "What game are you playing?"

"No game," Sheriff Circe says, stepping out from behind the desk. "Just some movie magic, if you will." She rubs her chin. "Now, let's see. What would make a good story? A showdown? A stampede?"

Circe snaps her fingers. "I know how to draw out the action! I'll give you a head start to get out of town."

If Wonder Woman plays along with Circe's game, turn to page 49.

If Wonder Woman is through playing, turn to page 60.

Wonder Woman thinks of the film crew transformed into pigs. She'll have to find a way to beat Circe at her own game.

"Fine," the hero says. "What do you want me to do?"

Circe grins. "Your horse is tied up outside."

"A horse?" Diana asks.

"That's right," replies Circe. "No cheating. No flying." Circe pulls out a pocket watch. "I'll give you a five minute head start before I send a posse after you."

Wonder Woman steps outside. She spots the hitching post, but it's empty. There's no horse. She walks around the post and bumps into something. A horse whinnies nearby, but she doesn't see it. Confused, Diana reaches out and touches something big and warm.

"An invisible horse just like my Invisible Jet." She shakes her head. Now she knows how others feel when they bump into her aircraft. "Very funny, Circe."

Turn to page 51.

Wonder Woman climbs onto the invisible horse and rides out of town. If she thought she received strange looks walking into town, she gets stranger ones now as she rides out.

Once out of town, Wonder Woman guides her horse toward the wooded hills a couple of miles away. The hero is about halfway there when she looks behind her. A large dust cloud blooms just outside of town. It seems Sheriff Circe has already sent a posse after her.

"Giddy-up!" Wonder Woman says, coaxing her invisible steed into a gallop.

When Diana reaches the hills, she spots a narrow trail leading into the forest. It looks like the perfect place to lose her pursuers. Then again, Wonder Woman doesn't like running from a fight. Part of her wants to circle around, ride back into town, and face Circe once and for all.

If Wonder Woman takes the trail, turn to page 52.
If Wonder Woman circles around, turn to page 56.

Wonder Woman gallops up the wooded trail. When she reaches the top of a large hill, she looks back down at the posse. A rider with a big white hat leads the group up the trail after her. It's Circe.

Diana follows the path over the hill and down into a large valley. Thundering hooves grow ever louder as her pursuers close the gap behind her.

When Wonder Woman enters the valley, she sees that it's filled with bison. The large herd of shaggy beasts grazes on the lush grass beyond.

"Perhaps I'll gather my own posse," she says.

Wonder Woman carefully rides her horse through the thick herd. The large creatures aren't alarmed as she makes her way to the other side of the valley.

"Maybe an invisible horse is a good idea after all," Wonder Woman says.

When the hero reaches the far side of the valley, she brings her horse to a stop. She turns and sees Circe and her posse enter the other side.

"Now it's time for a stampede," Diana says. She kicks her horse forward, running back toward the bison. But the herd doesn't budge.

"All right," Diana says. "An invisible horse is a bad idea after all."

In the meantime, Circe's posse charges through the valley. Unlike Wonder Woman's horse, their steeds do frighten the bison, making them run toward Diana.

"I better stop them quick," the hero says, raising her arms above her head. The Amazon warrior strikes her magic bracelets together.

BOOOOOOOM!

The bison snort in surprise. Their eyes widen as they gallop away from Diana—and back toward the posse. The ground shakes beneath the hundreds of thundering hooves.

Wonder Woman gallops after the stampeding herd. The bison gain speed as they close in on the posse. The men in the posse scramble to turn their horses around and escape the herd.

Turn the page.

"Get back here!" Circe orders. "A few bison never hurt anybody."

The men don't listen. They gallop up the trail leading out of the valley.

Then Circe's horse gets spooked like the others. It runs back up the trail after them. The frightened bison thunder after her.

Diana urges her invisible horse to gallop faster. She weaves it through the stampeding herd as they charge up the hill.

She catches up with Circe near the top of the hill. As the bison rush up the trail past her, Circe's horse backs toward the edge of a cliff. Frightened, it rears up on its hind legs.

"Ahhh!" Circe screams as she falls backward off the horse.

Wonder Woman unclips her golden lasso and twirls it above her head. She flings it toward Circe as she goes over the edge of the cliff. The lasso loops around the sorceress before she plummets to the jagged rocks below.

"Ugh, how embarrassing," Circe says as she's being hauled up over the edge. "I suppose you think I owe you one now." She blows a strand of purple hair from her face. "And that I'll simply restore the movie crew on principle."

"What do you think?" Wonder Woman asks. "Remember, the magic lasso compels you to tell the truth."

"Of course you think that," Circe says. "But lasso or not, you have to admit that my movie magic is much better than theirs."

"I'll agree with that," Wonder Woman says with a nod. "But you're still turning them back into humans."

Circe sighs. "Fine."

THE END

To follow another path, turn to page 15.

Wonder Woman spots a huge boulder beside the trail. She rides her horse behind it and waits for the posse to pass. Once the last cowboy rides by, Diana gallops back toward town.

"Let's see how brave Circe is without her posse," Wonder Woman says.

The hero rides into town and ties her horse to a hitching rail. She pets its invisible muzzle one last time before walking out into the street. The town seems deserted. Only a few townsfolk watch from the sidewalks.

"Circe!" Wonder Woman shouts. "Come out and face me!"

The sound of one person clapping fills the air. Circe applauds as she steps out from behind one of the buildings.

"Well done, princess," Circe says. "You chose to have a western showdown. Classic!"

Circe steps into the center of the dusty street. She rests her hands on the two six-shooters on her hips.

"But you seem to be missing something," the villain says.

The sorceress waves a hand, and Wonder Woman now wears a holster with a pair of six-shooters.

Diana folds her arms. "I don't need these weapons to defeat you."

"Well you'd better try," says Circe. "That's how this movie goes."

Wonder Woman sighs and rolls her eyes. Then, with lightning speed, she reaches for the six-shooters. She draws the weapons and is surprised when they turn into venomous snakes.

HISSSS! HISSSSSSS!

Diana throws the snakes to the ground, and they slither away.

"You should've seen your face," Circe says, doubling over in laughter.

The villain finally settles down and points to her own six-shooters. "You're right, though. I don't need these weapons either."

Turn the page.

Circe pretends to draw the six-shooters but points her fingers instead. ***TZZAP! TZZAP!*** Purple bolts of dark magic shoot from her fingertips.

Wonder Woman barely has enough time to raise her arms in defense. The bolts bounce off the Amazon's magic bracelets.

Circe continues to fire, and Wonder Woman crouches as she deflects more of the deadly blasts. Unfortunately, some of the bolts hit the town instead. Townsfolk run and scream as a building goes up in flames.

"What kind of hero are you?" asks Circe. "Setting a town on fire."

Wonder Woman runs off the street and leaps onto a building. She runs across the rooftops toward the nearby train station.

TZZAP! TZZAP! Circe continues to shoot dark magic her way.

When Diana spots what she's looking for, she pulls the lasso from her hip. She twirls it over her head and sends it flying.

The end of the magic rope latches onto a giant water tower. Wonder Woman leaps into the air and pulls the rope with all her might.

KRAK! One of the tower's legs breaks, and the tower falls over.

WHOOOOOSH!

The water tower smashes to the ground and empties itself down the city street. The raging floodwaters put out the fires when they crash into the building. But the runaway current also washes away the nearby sheriff—Circe!

Wonder Woman runs back along the rooftops, trying to keep up with the swept away sorceress. She twirls her lasso and tosses it into the flood. Diana digs her boots into the edge of a roof as she pulls against the current. Bit by bit, she hauls Circe from the water. The sorceress is out cold.

"This turned out to be a good movie," Wonder Woman says to Circe. "Too bad you slept through the ending."

THE END

To follow another path, turn to page 15.

"I give up," Wonder Woman says.

Circe's eyes widen. "What?"

"If I'm the big, mean outlaw," Diana raises her hands over her head, "then I'm turning myself in. I surrender . . . *Sheriff.*"

Circe scowls and crosses her arms. "Well, that doesn't make for a very exciting story, does it?"

Diana shrugs. "I wouldn't know. This is your movie, remember? I'm just playing a part."

The sorceress sighs and shakes her head. "Fine." She snatches a ring of keys from the desk and storms toward the back of the building. "This way then."

Wonder Woman follows Sheriff Circe toward the jail cells in back. Circe unlocks one of the metal doors and swings it open. Diana steps inside the cell and turns around.

"I'll just wait for my trial then," Wonder Woman says with a sly smile.

Circe glares at the hero. Then she throws her head back and laughs.

"You're right about playing a part in my movie, Diana dear," Circe says. "But if I don't like how you're playing, maybe I'll just change the channel."

BAM!

When Circe slams the cell door shut, a flash of light blinds Wonder Woman. When her vision clears, she finds herself in a different place entirely.

"Zeus almighty," Diana says as she looks around.

Wonder Woman no longer stands in a western jail cell but in a small futuristic chamber. An evacuated city appears through a large window in front of her. The Amazon warrior looks down on skyscrapers as if she stands inside a towering building.

Diana also notices that she no longer wears her western boots and hat. Instead she dons a helmet and a sleek uniform. Wires and tubes attach to her arms and legs.

Turn the page.

Wonder Woman raises an arm to examine the wires more closely. When she does, a giant robotic arm appears in the window in front of her. The robot hand opens and closes as Diana opens and closes her hand.

"I'm controlling a giant robot," she says in amazement. "From the inside."

Diana moves her legs, and she feels the floor shake as the robot moves forward. She turns her head, and the view in the window changes. She controls the giant machine's every move.

BOOM! Her robot rocks to one side as something hits it—hard. The hero turns to see another robot moving in for another attack. The enemy robot throws a punch with a massive metal fist. Wonder Woman raises her arm, and her robot's arm blocks the blow.

"Hard to sit out *this* story, huh?" asks a familiar voice over a nearby speaker.

Diana spots Circe through a window on the other robot's head. The wicked sorceress wears a similar uniform as she controls the other robot.

Turn to page 64.

Distracted by the new science fiction world, Diana misses a kick from Circe's robot. The metallic foot slams into her robot's chest. She staggers backward, trying to keep her robot on its feet.

"I was trained to fight by the best warriors on Themyscira," Wonder Woman says. "But this is going to take some getting used to."

Wonder Woman blocks a punch from Circe's robot. Then she delivers a powerful backhand. Circe's robot spins as it flies backward.

BOOOM! It smashes through a skyscraper as it tumbles to the ground. Shattered glass and concrete shower the downed robot.

"That's more like it," Circe says as her robot gets to its feet and dusts itself off. Then it lowers its head and charges.

Wonder Woman sidesteps, and her robot does the same. Circe's robot plows past, missing her completely. The enemy robot skids to a stop and spins back toward Diana.

"You can't escape me," Circe growls. Her robot reaches out to grab her opponent.

Wonder Woman reaches up, and her robot's hands come into view. She makes her robot catch the hands of Circe's robot. The two giant machines push against each other, locked in battle. The floor rumbles beneath Diana's feet as her robot's heels dig into the street below.

BEEP! BEEP! BEEP! BEEP!

An alarm sounds inside the chamber. Diana glances around at the many gauges and dials surrounding her. She finally notices a shrinking bar of light.

"Oh no!" she says. "This thing is almost out of power."

Then her entire world rocks as Circe makes her robot head-butt Wonder Woman's.

WHAM!

Wonder Woman's robot loses its footing. It stumbles and falls backward into another building.

Turn the page.

KRASH!

Diana's view is filled with raining glass and metal beams as she crashes through the building. Then her view quickly shifts to open sky as her robot falls onto its back.

Diana tries to rise, but Circe's robot dashes forward with lightning speed. It slams a foot on the chest of Diana's robot, pinning it to the ground. Circe's robot presses down on Wonder Woman's robot. Inside the chamber, the structure creaks and moans. More lights flash and alarms sound.

"This machine can't take much more of this punishment," Wonder Woman says. "And it's using up what's left of its power."

Then she spots a large red button labeled, *EJECT.*

If Wonder Woman ejects, turn to page 67.
If Wonder Woman finds more power, turn to page 70.

Wonder Woman reaches out and presses the red button. Wires and hoses disconnect from her uniform, and a hatch opens above. The floor springboards beneath her feet, and she shoots out of the robot's head. The Amazon warrior somersaults in midair before landing atop a pile of rubble.

Circe's robot looms over her. "You can't escape that easily, Princess," Circe says. Her robot raises a foot and brings it down toward the hero. Luckily, Wonder Woman dives out of the way at the last minute.

"I don't need a giant robot to defeat you," Diana says. She grabs onto the robot's foot and scrambles up its leg.

"What are you doing?" Circe asks.

Wonder Woman climbs higher and smashes through the robot's metal skin with one punch. She reaches in and rips out wires and hoses.

TZZZ! TZZZ! Sparks fly and liquid squirts from the hoses.

Turn the page.

Circe's robot stiffens. "I can't move my leg," she shouts.

The villain's robot reaches down, trying to swat Diana off its leg. Wonder Woman dodges the hand as it passes. Then she leaps up and grabs onto its wrist. She scrambles higher up the arm and punches a second hole through the metal. She pulls out more hoses and cables.

"My arm," Circe cries. "I can't move it either!"

Wonder Woman doesn't stop. She leaps across the robot and latches onto its other arm. She tears through the metal and inflicts the same kind of damage.

TZZZZ! TZZZ! TZZZZ! More sparks and fluid pour out.

"What have you done to me?" asks Circe. "I can't move at all!"

Diana runs up the robot's chest. She clasps her hands together and swings a double fist at the robot's chin.

BAM!

The robot head flies off of its body. **CLANK!** **CLANK-CLANK!** With Circe still inside, it bounces to a stop atop a pile of rubble.

Wonder Woman jumps down and lands upon the head. Circe angrily presses her own eject button, but nothing happens. Then she pounds at the clear window.

"Get me out of here!" she demands.

Wonder Woman crosses her arms. "You can get yourself out," she says. "When you return us to our own world and restore the movie crew."

Circe pounds once more before finally giving up. "Oh, all right," she says with a sigh. "But you have to admit that my robots were much better than that dumb mechanical Cyclops."

"Perhaps," says Wonder Woman. "But if I were you, I'd stick to watching movies instead of making them." She shakes her head at the sorceress. "You just get too into your work."

THE END

To follow another path, turn to page 15.

Controlling her own giant robot, Wonder Woman tries to pry Circe's foot from atop her.

WRRRRRR! TZZZ! TZZZ! Motors whir and circuits spark, but she can't budge it.

"I have to find a way to get more power," Diana says.

KRAK! KRUNCH! KRAK! Her robot's metal shell begins to give under Circe's weight.

Wonder Woman glances around, looking for anything to help. She finally reaches out her robot arm and grabs a nearby power line.

TZZZZZ! TZZZZ! Sparks fly as electricity courses through the giant robot. It also flows into Circe's robot.

"Yeow!" Circe shouts as the shock hits her. Her robot flies backward.

Wonder Woman grits her teeth as the electricity flows through her body. Even in this strange movie world, she has superhuman strength. The shock doesn't harm her, and she watches as the power levels rise in her robot.

Once her robot is fully charged, Wonder Woman drops the wire. She makes the robot push itself off the ground, and it gets to its feet with lightning speed. She moves the robot toward Circe and performs a spin kick.

WHACK!

Circe's robot flies back, crashing into another skyscraper.

"As much as I'm enjoying this battle," Wonder Woman says, "I need to end it quickly."

The hero moves back to the power line and grabs the loose end. Paying no mind to the shock, Diana has her robot pull the line from the poles and wind it into a coil.

"This isn't my magic lasso," Wonder Woman says. "But it should still do the trick."

Meanwhile, Circe's robot gets to its feet. The sorceress screams in frustration as her robot charges toward Wonder Woman.

"I'll crush you!" Circe shouts.

Turn the page.

As Circe closes in, Diana's robot swings the electrical wire over its head like a giant lasso. Then it tosses the wire, encircling Circe's robot.

TZZZZZZZZZ! The robot smokes and shudders as electricity courses through it.

"Yeow!" Circe cries out from the shock.

Finally, the villain's robot falls backward, snapping the wire. ***BOOOM!*** It lands flat on its back.

When the dust clears, Wonder Woman moves her robot closer and leans down. She peers through Circe's window to see that the sorceress is out cold. Diana makes her robot sit down beside Circe's.

"Sleep well, Circe," Diana tells her. "I'll be here to take you to justice when you wake up."

THE END

To follow another path, turn to page 15.

FLASH!

With a burst of light, Wonder Woman suddenly finds herself in a strange situation. She sits in the back of a limousine with three other people. That's not so odd—she's been in limousines before. The strange part is that they are all in black and white. They aren't just wearing black-and-white clothing, but everything is in black and white. There are no colors at all.

"Circe used her dark magic to put me inside an old movie," Diana says to herself.

"I'm sorry, dear," says the woman sitting across from her. "What was your name again?"

"I'm Diana," says Wonder Woman.

The woman wears a white evening gown made of several long strips of material. A matching turban sits atop her head.

"I'm Millicent Mumford," says the woman. She points to the thin man sitting on her left. "This is William Salvania."

Turn the page.

The thin man wears a tuxedo and gives Diana a small nod. "Pleased to meet you."

Millicent gestures to the man on her right. He is a stout man with scruffy hair and a plain gray suit. "And this is Harold T. Vulfman."

"Good evening," the man says in a German accent.

"Hello," Diana replies. She looks down and notices that she wears a long black evening gown. She looks back to the others. "Where are we going?"

"Why, to a dinner party, of course," Millicent says, pointing to their destination.

Diana sees that the limousine is driving up a long and winding driveway. An eerie manor stands at the end, atop a steep hill. Black clouds surround the upper floors.

KRACK-BOOM! A jagged bolt of lightning cuts through the night.

"Oh, boy," Wonder Woman says to herself. "What is Circe up to now?"

When Diana and the party guests arrive, they are ushered into a large dining room. They each take seats along a grand dining room table.

"Welcome," says an all too familiar voice. The chair at the head of the table spins around to face them. Dressed in an evening gown of her own, Circe smiles at everyone. "Welcome honored guests!"

"What game are you playing, Circe?" Diana asks her.

"Why, only the most exciting game around," Circe says. "The game of survival!"

Circe waves a hand and the massive doors to the dining room slam shut. *BAM!*

Then, one by one, shutters swing shut over all the windows. *KLAK! KLAK! KLAK! KLAK!* The three guests leap to their feet in surprise. Diana remains seated.

"All right, Circe," Wonder Woman says. "You proved your point. You can create a whole movie world with your dark magic."

Turn to page 77.

"Oh, but I'm not finished, Princess," Circe says. "If you want to save that movie crew, you'll have to finish *my* movie." She raises both hands dramatically. "And survive a night in the haunted manor!"

KRACK-BOOM! Thunder roars outside.

"This is between us," Wonder Woman says. She points to the guests. "Let these others go, and I'll play your silly game."

"Oh, no," Circe says, shaking her finger. "Everyone has a role to play." She waves a hand toward the nearby fireplace. The entire structure moves aside to reveal a secret passageway. "Now, let the fun begin!"

If Wonder Woman enters the secret passage, turn to page 78.
If Wonder Woman refuses to play her role, turn to page 100.

Wonder Woman springs from her chair and rushes toward Circe. But the sorceress vanishes in a puff of gray smoke.

"No cheating," echoes Circe's voice.

Diana sighs. "Fine," she says, moving toward the secret passage. She grabs a torch from the wall and lights it using the fireplace.

"It sure is dark down there," Millicent says nervously.

William dabs his forehead with a white handkerchief. "Perhaps one of us should stay here," he suggests.

"There's no telling what Circe has planned for us," Wonder Woman says. "We'll have a better chance if we stay together and face it as one."

"I'm not scared," Harold says. He peers down the dark corridor and cracks his knuckles. "Let's get on with it."

With torch in hand, Diana leads the way down the dimly lit passage. Harold walks next to her, while William and Millicent bring up the rear.

The group rounds a corner and enters a large room with marble floors and walls. Several suits of armor line the walls. The knightly displays hold large shields and sharp swords.

Harold marches up to one of the suits. "I'll feel better with one of these swords," he says.

He grabs one of the swords from the displays. "This'll do nicely," he says as he examines the sharp blade. But suddenly, the suit of armor reaches up and snatches it back. "What the?" Harold asks.

Then *all* of the suits come to life! They each raise their swords and move in toward the group.

"Get behind me," orders Wonder Woman.

The hero raises her arms and blocks the sword strike with her silver bracelets. Then she elbows a knight right in the faceplate. The empty helmet flies away. There's no one in the armor!

The headless suit stumbles back toward a pillar. **KLANK! RATTLE! KRASH!** The armor pieces fall apart when they hit the hard marble.

Turn the page.

Wonder Woman jumps over a striking sword and ducks under another. Then she dodges three more as she dives for the fallen suit of armor.

SWISH! SWISH! SWISH! The sharp blades narrowly miss her as she slides along the floor. She grabs the sword from the ground and leaps to her feet. She charges the advancing knights.

KLINK! KLANK! KLINK! The group stays behind Diana as she fights off the suits of armor. Each suit falls apart when she lands a solid blow. Soon, there are no more to fight. The chamber is littered with broken armor.

Wonder Woman throws down her sword. "Come on," she orders. "Let's see what else that sorceress has in store for us."

Diana leads the group out of the chamber and into another long corridor. They pass several paintings hung along the hallway. Many of them are portraits, including one of Circe herself. In the painting, the sorceress wears a long dark gown. Her eyes also seem to follow them as they move down the corridor.

Turn to page 82.

"Very funny, Circe," Wonder Woman says.

When they reach the end, the hallway veers off to the left, while a set of stairs leads downward on the right. Wonder Woman stops and peers at the dark flight of stairs.

William crosses his arms. "Now should we split up?"

Diana shakes her head. "I don't think so."

"I don't want to go down there," Millicent says with wide eyes.

"Which way do we go?" asks Harold.

If Wonder Woman chooses the stairs, turn to page 83.
If Wonder Woman continues down the hallway, turn to page 90.

"Wait here," Wonder Woman says. "I'll go first to see if it's safe." She grabs another torch and steps into the stairwell.

Diana takes a few steps down but can't see what's at the bottom of the stairs. The torch isn't strong enough, and no light comes from below.

"Maybe this isn't the way to go," she says, shaking her head.

Wonder Woman turns around and walks up the stairs. Then suddenly, the steps collapse and form a long ramp. Diana skids down the flattened stairs as if it were a giant slide.

FLASH!

With a burst of purple light, Wonder Woman lands on something soft. She opens her eyes to see that everything is in color again. She now wears a leather jacket and a racing helmet. She also discovers she's strapped into the driver's seat of a moving race car!

Diana takes the steering wheel and jerks it to the left to avoid crashing into another car.

Turn the page.

"Where has that sorceress put me now?" Wonder Woman asks. She seems to be in the middle of a race through city streets.

Diana lets off the gas pedal and her car begins to slow. Just then, a green car pulls up next to her. The tinted window lowers, and Circe is driving!

"Fancy a race, Diana?" Circe asks.

"No, I do not," Wonder Woman replies. "Racing through a city like this is reckless."

Circe waves her away. "I created this world. No one's going to get hurt but you." She flashes a sly smile. "Besides, if you win, you go home."

Circe rolls up the window and takes off. Her car pulls away, moving up the pack of street racers.

"I accept your challenge," Wonder Woman says. Then she grips the wheel tightly and floors the gas pedal.

VROOM!

Turn to page 86.

Diana's car zooms forward. She jerks the wheel left and right as she weaves in between the other cars. She slowly moves up the pack as they fly over bridges and skid around corners.

Diana pulls the hand brake as her car drifts around another corner. Then she spots Circe's car. It's only a block away. Wonder Woman narrows her eyes as she presses the gas.

BLINK! BLINK! A flashing light on her car's computer screen gets Wonder Woman's attention. It shows her as a yellow dot on a map of the city. Circe is a green dot, much closer to the finish line. The race is almost over, and Circe is about to win.

Wonder Woman looks back up and spots a truck with a flat trailer up ahead. The trailer is angled up, almost like a ramp.

"Perfect!" the hero says to herself.

Wonder Woman steps on the gas and aims for the trailer. Her car races up the trailer and flies into the air over Circe's car. It lands hard on the street in front of the villain.

Diana can see Circe's scowling face in the rearview mirror. The sorceress is not happy with Wonder Woman being in first place.

Diana concentrates on the road. "Let's get this race over with," she says to herself. She is almost at the finish line.

KRACK! A jagged rock shoots up from the street ahead of her.

"Mighty Atlas!" Wonder Woman shouts. Her tires screech as she barely steers clear of the enormous boulder.

KRACK! KRACK-KRACK!

Three more rocks erupt from the street. Diana swerves past each of them.

"Circe can't stand losing," Wonder Woman says. "So she must have decided to cheat."

Diana grips the wheel harder. She is not going to let Circe win.

KRAAACK! The biggest jagged rock so far shoots up from below.

Turn the page.

Wonder Woman jerks the wheel and steers clear of most of it. Unfortunately, one tire catches the rock, and her car launches into the air. It spirals as it flies and ends up on its roof when it hits the ground. Sparks fly as it scrapes down the road.

"I'm not out yet," Wonder Woman says.

As the hero's car slides toward the finish line, Wonder Woman climbs out the window. She scrambles onto the underbelly of her car and rides it like a giant snowboard. Even though it's upside down, Diana's car crosses the finish line first. Spectators cheer as camera flashes explode around her.

Circe's car skids to a stop beside her.

"I'm impressed, Princess," the villain says. "And a deal's a deal. I'll restore the movie crew and transport you back."

"Thank you, Circe," says Wonder Woman. "I'm glad to hear you're willing to hold up your end of the bargain."

Wonder Woman hops off her car and leans into the villain's car. "But before you do . . . ," she glances around. "Want to race again?"

A mischievous grin spreads across Circe's face. "I thought you'd never ask." She snaps her fingers and Wonder Woman's car is restored.

Diana climbs in and buckles up. "But no cheating this time," she says.

Circe rolls her eyes. "Oh, all right."

THE END

To follow another path, turn to page 15.

"Follow me," Wonder Woman says. "Forget the stairs for now. Everyone stay together."

She leads them down the new corridor. This one isn't filled with portraits like the last. It has silver-framed mirrors on either side instead. Wonder Woman freezes in front of the first mirror she comes to.

"What in the world?" she asks. In the mirror, Diana no longer wears her black evening gown. Instead, she wears her usual Amazonian attire.

"I don't understand," says Millicent. Her reflection shows a mummy looking back at her. "Does this show the future? Am I going to be in an accident?"

"This is dreadful," says William. He sees a winged vampire in his mirror.

"Hey, look at me." Harold grins as he stares at a werewolf in the mirror. "Who's a good boy?" he laughs. "Who's a good boy?"

"These are just more of Circe's games," says Wonder Woman. "Let's keep moving."

The group spills into a large chamber at the end of the corridor. The round room is ringed with burning torches, and an enormous ball of thick rope is positioned in the center.

Wonder Woman steps closer to the giant knot. "Great Alexander," she says. "What kind of puzzle is this?"

Harold marches forward and grabs at the rope. He can barely get his huge hands around the thick cord. "It won't budge," he says as he tugs at the knot.

"You didn't say please," echoes a familiar voice.

The knot unwinds in a flash. It wasn't a rope but a giant snake instead. The serpent flicks its forked tongue at Diana and the others. "Did you miss me?" it asks with Circe's voice.

With lightning speed, the Circe snake coils itself around Wonder Woman and lifts her off the ground. The hero struggles to break free as the snake squeezes tighter.

Turn the page.

"You're powerless against me," says the Circe snake. "Just admit it. I won."

"Never," grunts Wonder Woman. "Because you left us a clue. In your mirrors."

There's a flash of light and now Wonder Woman is wearing her usual uniform. She uses all of her Amazonian strength to break free of the snake's grip.

The Circe snake strikes, but Wonder Woman is too quick. She dodges the large fangs and punches the beast with both fists. **_POW!_**

Diana hovers over the others as the Circe snake recoils from the blow.

"The mirrors showed all of us," Wonder Woman says. "Bring out your true power."

Suddenly, Millicent's dress and turban unravel and wrap all over her body, turning her into a mummy. William grows fangs and sprouts large bat wings, becoming a giant winged vampire. And Harold rips through his shirt and coat as he transforms into a werewolf.

The three monsters join the fight against the giant snake. The vampire hovers in front of it, distracting it. Strips of the mummy's bandages wrap around the snake's body. And the werewolf leaps onto the snake's back and rakes its scales with sharp claws.

"How dare you turn my monsters against me!" shouts the Circe snake.

"Do you yield?" asks Wonder Woman.

"Never!" replies the snake.

The Circe snake moves in for another strike, but Wonder Woman spin kicks the side of its head. The snake wobbles as the three monsters continue their relentless attack.

Circe growls in frustration. "Fine!"

FLASH!

With a burst of light, Wonder Woman finds herself back on the beach with Circe. The movie crew is back to normal.

"What happened?" the director asks, walking up to the Amazon.

Turn the page.

Wonder Woman points to the sorceress. "Oh, someone was just telling me about movie magic."

"No, I mean what happened to my beautiful Polyphemus?" The dismayed director points to the smashed mechanical Cyclops. The sand is littered with bits of metal and rubber.

Wonder Woman cringes. "I forgot all about that." Then she tosses her lasso around Circe. "A little help, if you please?"

Circe rolls her eyes. "Oh, all right."

She snaps her fingers and the mechanical Cyclops is restored in a flash of purple light. It once again looms over the beach with its huge wooden club.

"Thank you," says Wonder Woman. "And a great example of movie magic, by the way."

Circe is taken aback by the compliment.

"Why, thank *you*," she replies.

THE END

To follow another path, turn to page 15.

"I accept your challenge," Diana says.

"Excellent," Circe replies with a grin.

The sorceress snaps her fingers, and Diana is hit with a flash of light. When her eyes clear, she finds herself on a barren planet. Only alien scrub brush and rocky hills dot the landscape.

Then Wonder Woman spots her opponent. A little alien runs toward her, his green skin glistening beneath the planet's two suns. He pumps his four arms as he runs toward her.

But something is not quite right. After a dozen heartbeats, the alien is still running toward her. Wonder Woman realizes he just seemed small because Circe placed him so far away. As the alien approaches, Diana can see that he is actually massive.

"I knew Circe had something up her sleeve," Wonder Woman says.

As her opponent nears, he towers over the Amazon. He doesn't stop and immediately takes a swing at her with two massive arms.

Turn the page.

"We don't have to fight," Wonder Woman says as she ducks out of the way.

The alien doesn't answer. Instead, it tries to backhand her. Diana dodges that attack too.

"Well, if you won't listen to reason," Wonder Woman says. She balls up a fist and punches the alien in the jaw. It feels as if she punched a brick wall. The alien doesn't seem to notice.

"Great Hera," she says with surprise.

Wonder Woman is so surprised that she doesn't notice the two green fists coming at her.

POW!

The blow sends her flying far across the landscape. She finally skids to a stop near a crop of alien trees.

"This being has the strength of Superman," she says to herself. "And Circe knows it."

Wonder Woman looks around for any kind of weapon. She only wears her starship captain's uniform and doesn't have any of her usual gear.

As the alien marches toward her, Wonder Woman spots a thin root. She pulls a length of it out of the ground.

"It's not my lasso, but it'll be good enough," she says.

The alien marches closer, but Wonder Woman can't break the root free from the nearby tree. It's as if everything on this alien world is as strong as her.

Suddenly, a nearby alien tree whips forward. Diana barely dives out of the way as its branches try to grab her.

"So much for using a root," Diana says. "It looks as if everything on this planet is out to get me. Well played, Circe."

Her alien opponent finally marches up to her. He growls as he tries to pound her with four massive fists. Wonder Woman dives clear as they strike the ground.

BAM-BAM-BAM-BAM! A massive dust cloud erupts from the soil.

Turn the page.

Diana uses the distraction to hide behind the large alien tree. As she watches her opponent look for her, she notices him standing over the exposed root. She gets an idea.

"Looking for me?!" she shouts as she steps out from behind the tree.

Before the brute can attack, Wonder Woman runs straight toward him. Then, at the last minute, she dives for the ground and skids between his legs.

WHOOSH!

The alien tries to grab her, but all four of its arms miss.

Once on the other side of him, Diana turns and pulls at the root in the ground. Like before, the tree whips toward her. Only this time, the alien is in the way. The branches wrap around him like a cage.

The alien tries to break free, but he's trapped in the intertwined branches.

Wonder Woman stands and dusts herself off. "All right, I won your challenge," she says. "Now, let's see if you'll keep your word, Circe."

In a flash of light, Wonder Woman finds that she is back on the beach. Circe stands beside her, and the movie crew is back to normal.

"I'm impressed, Princess," Circe says.

Wonder Woman crosses her arms. "I should take you back to Themyscira for what you've done to those people."

Circe grins. "You'll have to catch me first." Then she snaps her fingers and disappears.

THE END

To follow another path, turn to page 15.

Wonder Woman crosses her arms. "No."

"What?!" Circe asks.

"You heard me," Diana says. "I refuse to play games with people's lives."

The sorceress grins. "Oh, but you forget. I created these characters. They are my lives to play with."

Circe snaps and Millicent screams. Her gown and turban come alive. The strips of cloth slither around her body like flat white snakes.

Millicent tries to scream again, but the cloth from the turban wraps around her face. The strips from her dress encircle her arms and legs. Soon, Millicent isn't Millicent anymore. She's a mummy!

Next, Harold doubles over in pain. His jacket rips down the back and thick brown fur pushes through. His screams turn to snarls and growls as his hands and feet stretch and deform. Once completely changed, Harold looks at Wonder Woman with wild eyes. He's a werewolf.

William grins at Diana as two sharp fangs appear in his mouth. His ears stretch to floppy points and his nose flattens. Fleshy bat wings sprout from his back. His eyes seem to flash as he stares at the Amazon with hunger. William becomes a huge vampire.

The werewolf is the first to attack. He leaps toward Diana, and she pushes out of her chair.

POW! With a single kick, she sends the beast flying across the room.

The vampire is next. With superhuman speed, he flies up to Wonder Woman and tries to bite her neck. Luckily, the Amazon warrior is faster. She blocks the attack with her wrist.

TING!

The vampire hisses as his sharp fangs bounce off her silver bracelet. She then reaches over the vampire and grabs him by the back of his neck. She flips him over her head and sends him flying. **CRASH!** He collides with the recovering werewolf.

Turn the page.

Wonder Woman turns to confront Circe, but the hero is suddenly trapped. Long strips of cloth wrap around her, pinning her arms to her side. It's the mummy!

More strips unravel from the creature's arms and wrap around Wonder Woman. They squeeze tighter and tighter.

The vampire and werewolf take the opportunity to attack again. They leap onto the bound hero, trying to bring her down. She tries to shrug them off, but they hold on tight. They snarl, claw, and bite at her.

Luckily, Diana can still move her legs. She runs as fast as she can toward one of the shuttered windows. Taking all three monsters with her, she leaps into the air and crashes through it.

SMASH!!!

Wonder Woman and the three creatures tumble though the night air along with broken glass and splintered wood. They land hard and spill out onto the wet lawn.

Diana rolls free from their clutches. She springs to her feet and readies for battle as the monsters surround her. They growl and inch closer with pointed fangs and razor-sharp claws.

Buckets of rain pour from above, and wicked lightning bolts snake across the sky

KRACK-BOOM!

With the last bright flash of lightning, Wonder Woman suddenly finds herself sitting in a movie theater. She holds a large tub of popcorn and watches an old black-and-white movie on the screen. Diana sees herself on the screen facing off against the three movie monsters.

"So . . . what do you think?" Circe asks. The sorceress sits in the seat next to her. "I told you I could make my own movie magic."

Wonder Woman glances around the theater. The movie crew from before fills the seats around them. They are no longer pigs and seem to be enjoying the movie.

Turn the page.

"Very clever, Circe," Diana replies. "And I'm glad to see you changed the movie crew back."

Circe shrugs and munches on a handful of popcorn. "Well, someone had to show them what real movie magic looked like."

Wonder Woman chuckles. "I'll give you that," she says. "But you know . . . I'm still turning you in to the authorities when the show is over."

"In that case . . . ," Circe begins. She snaps her fingers and vanishes in a puff of purple smoke. "I'll see you in the sequel, Princess," her voice echoes.

Wonder Woman shakes her head and smiles. Then she grabs another handful of popcorn and enjoys the rest of the movie.

THE END

To follow another path, turn to page 15.

AUTHOR

Michael Anthony Steele has been in the entertainment industry for more than 25 years writing for television, movies, and video games. He has authored more than 110 books for exciting characters and brands including: Batman, Superman, Green Lantern, Spider-Man, Shrek, Scooby-Doo, LEGO City, Garfield, Winx Club, *Night at the Museum*, and *The Penguins of Madagascar*. Mr. Steele lives on a ranch in Texas, but he enjoys meeting his readers when he visits schools and libraries all over the country.

ILLUSTRATOR

Omar Lozano lives in Monterrey, Mexico. He has always been crazy for illustration and is constantly on the lookout for awesome things to draw. In his free time, he watches lots of movies, reads fantasy and sci-fi books, and draws! Omar has worked for Marvel, DC, IDW, Capstone, and several other publishing companies.

GLOSSARY

bullhorn (BUL-horn)—an electronic device used to make a person's voice louder

catapult (KAT-uh-puhlt)—a large weapon, similar to a slingshot, used in the past to fire objects over castle walls

crossbow (KRAWS-boh)—a weapon based on the bow and arrow

mythology (mi-THOL-uh-jee)—a collection of myths

phoenix (FEE-niks)—a mythical bird that can burn up and then rise again from the ashes renewed

portal (POHR-tuhl)—a large, impressive opening or entrance

sequel (SEE-kwuhl)—a story that carries an existing one forward

sorceress (SOR-sur-uhss)—a woman with magical powers

stampede (stam-PEED)—a sudden wild rush of a frightened herd of animals

transform (transs-FORM)—to make a great change in something

transmission (transs-MISH-uhn)—a message or signal that is sent from one person or place to another

turban (TUR-buhn)—a head covering made by winding a long scarf around the head or around a cap

CIRCE

Species:
Olympian

Occupation:
Sorceress

Base:
Aeaea

Height:
5 feet 11 inches

Weight:
145 pounds

Eyes:
Blue

Hair:
Purple

Powers/Abilities:
Nearly limitless magical power, including the power
to transform mortal beings into animals. She also
has the power to project her voice, image, and
energy bolts over long distances.

Circe is an ancient sorceress who has a mischievous spirit and a flair for the dramatic. The villain practices the art of dark magic, though she's far from perfect at using it fully. Her magical abilities include changing people into animals, projecting her voice, firing magical energy blasts, and teleporting between dimensions. Over the millennia, Circe has taken many different forms in order to trick people into doing her bidding. One never knows where she might pop up next.

- Circe hates Wonder Woman and everything she stands for. She has spent a large amount of time plotting against the Amazon Princess and believes it's the hero's fault she has yet to become a villainous powerhouse.

- Circe loves nothing more than to humiliate others. That may be why animal transformation is one of her magical specialties. More often than not, those who cross her find themselves turned into pigs.

- Circe may have magic on her side, but Wonder Woman has a little magic of her own. The Amazon warrior's silver bracelets are the perfect defense against Circe's sorcery. They allow Wonder Woman to block magic, preventing damage and transformation.